MARIA

IRINI

Angelina Ballerina

Loves the Library

Based on the stories by Katharine Holabird
Based on the illustrations by Helen Craig

Ready-to-Read

Simon Spotlight
New York   London   Toronto   Sydney   New Delhi

SIMON SPOTLIGHT

An imprint of Simon & Schuster Children's Publishing Division

1230 Avenue of the Americas, New York, New York 10020

This Simon Spotlight edition December 2021

Illustrations by Mike Deas

For information about special discounts for bulk purchases, please contact Simon & Schuster Special Sales at

1-866-506-1949 or business@simonandschuster.com.

Manufactured in the United States of America 1021 LAK

10 9 8 7 6 5 4 3 2 1

ISBN 978-1-5344-9821-1 (hc)

ISBN 978-1-5344-9820-4 (pbk)

ISBN 978-1-5344-9822-8 (ebook)

Angelina Ballerina skipped
all the way to the
Chipping Cheddar Library.

She was excited to get
her first library card!

She could not wait
to discover some
wonderful new books!

"There are so many
beautiful books
at the library!"
Angelina said,
and Miss Fernsby nodded.

First, Angelina looked
for books about dancing.
She found two books she
wanted to read.

She was thrilled to find
a book about her favorite
dancer, Serena Silvertail!

Then Angelina looked for
books about her other
favorite things.

Her pile of books was
getting heavy.
Even so, Angelina found
more and more books
she wanted to read.

"I am sorry, Angelina,"
Miss Fernsby said.
"You can only borrow
five books at a time."

"Oh!"
Angelina said,
looking sad.

"Do not worry!"
Miss Fernsby said.
"You can come back for
more books next time!"

Angelina chose the
five books she wanted
to read first.
Then she danced all
the way home!

When she got home,
Angelina showed
her mother the *Mouseling
Cheddar Cheese Cookbook.*

Angelina and her mother had lots of fun trying some of the yummy new recipes!

Then Angelina read
to her sister Polly from
*Stories of Old Chipping
Cheddar.*

They loved learning
about their special little
village!

Later, Angelina went to
ballet class.
She kindly shared the
Serena Silvertail ballet
book with all her friends.

All the little ballerinas
practiced twirling
just like Serena Silvertail!

After class, Angelina
and Alice relaxed in
the garden.

They had fun
looking at the pictures
in a library book about art.
Then they made drawings!

Later, Angelina read
a funny pirate book
with her cousin Henry.

They pretended to be
pirates together!
"Ahoy!"
shouted Henry.

Angelina shared her
books with everyone.
Soon it was time
to bring the books
back to the library again.

"Did you enjoy the books?"
Miss Fernsby asked.
 "I loved them!"
Angelina said.

Then Angelina had more fun
finding five more books
to take home and read.

But Angelina was so excited
that she sat in the library
and read them all right away.
Happily, there were lots more
wonderful books to take home!